OLIVIA™
Goes to the Library

adapted by Lauren Forte
based on the episode written by
Kate Boutilier and Eryk Casemiro

illustrated by Jared Osterhold

Ready-to-Read

Simon Spotlight
New York   London   Toronto   Sydney   New Delhi

Based on the TV series OLIVIA™ as seen on Nickelodeon™

SIMON SPOTLIGHT
An imprint of Simon & Schuster Children's Publishing Division
1230 Avenue of the Americas, New York, New York 10020
For information about special discounts for bulk purchases, please contact Simon & Schuster Special Sales at
1-866-506-1949 or business@simonandschuster.com.
Manufactured in the United States of America 1013 LAK
First Edition 1 2 3 4 5 6 7 8 9 10
ISBN 978-1-4424-8478-8 (pbk)
ISBN 978-1-4424-8479-5 (hc)
ISBN 978-1-4424-8480-1 (eBook)

"What are you reading,
Olivia?" asks Ian.
"The Enchanted Pineapple
Princess,"
Olivia answers.

"Ready to go to the library?"
asks Dad.
"Our books are due back
today."

"But I am not done with mine," replies Olivia.
"We can renew it," says Dad.

"Hold on to your book,"
Dad tells Olivia.
"Ian, can you drop the rest
into the slot?"

"Can we listen to story time?" Olivia asks.
"Sure," says Dad.

Olivia puts her book down
next to her.

"'They lived happily ever after,'"
reads the storyteller at the end.

"That was almost as good as The Enchanted Pineapple Princess," Olivia tells him. "I do not know that one," he replies.

"I will show you," says Olivia. But the book is gone!

Olivia looks for the book,
but she cannot find it.

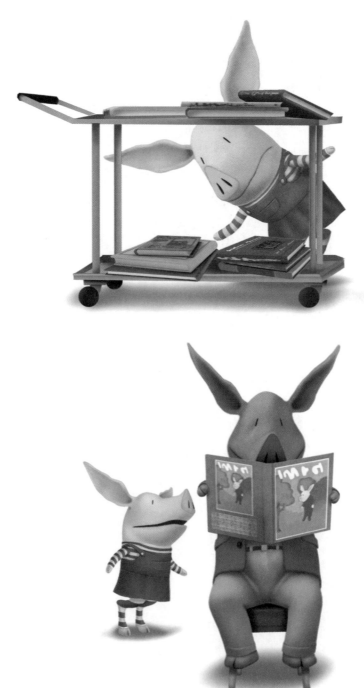

"Can I help you?"
asks the librarian.

"I left my book on a chair," says Olivia.
"Now it is missing."
"I will let you know if I see it," the librarian promises.

"Dad, have you seen my book?" Olivia asks.
Dad has not seen it.
Olivia keeps looking.

"Ian, want to go on an exciting adventure to look for my book?" asks Olivia. "That is not exciting, but okay," says Ian.

"I think I see it!" yells Olivia.

"Is it there?" asks Ian.

"No, but I did find Julian,"
Olivia says, giggling.

The storyteller is holding the book!
"I was about to read this for story time," he says.

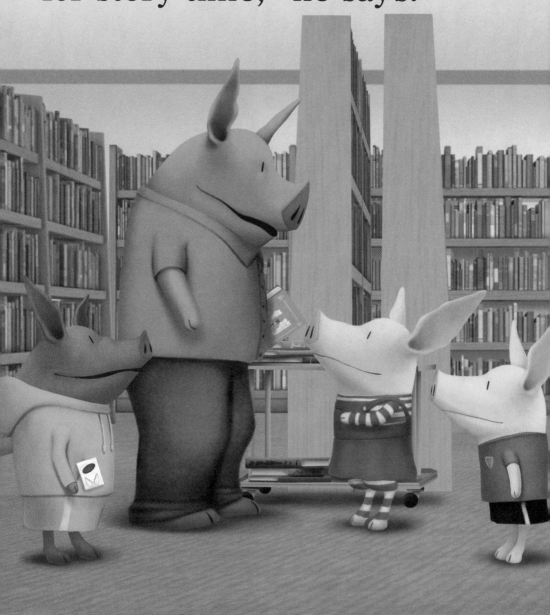

"Come listen, and you can check it out after. 'Once upon a time . . .'"

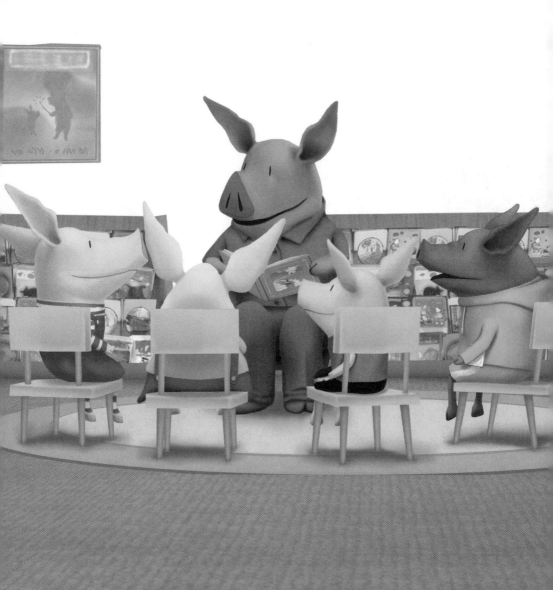

Olivia hears the story one more time before bed. "'They lived happily ever after,'" Mom reads. "Good night, Olivia!"